Princess Euphorbia

Vashti Farrer

Illustrated by
Nan Bodsworth

Supa
DOOPERS

sundance

Published by
Sundance Publishing
234 Taylor Street
Littleton, MA 01460

Copyright © text Vashti Farrer
Copyright © illustrations Nan Bodsworth
Project commissioned and managed by
Lorraine Bambrough-Kelly, The Writer's Style
Designed by Cath Lindsey/design rescue

First published 1997 by
Addison Wesley Longman Australia Pty Limited
95 Coventry Street
South Melbourne 3205 Australia
Exclusive United States Distribution: Sundance Publishing

ISBN 0-7608-1923-8

PRINTED IN CANADA

Contents

CHAPTER 1

Princess Euphorbia

There was once a king called Eglantine, who had a wife, Queen Gazania, and a daughter, the Princess Euphorbia. Now they were all perfectly normal, except for one thing: Princess Euphorbia's hair.

Princesses are meant to have long golden hair and blue eyes. They're also supposed to marry handsome princes, who ride dashing white horses and happen to dance superbly. However, Princess Euphorbia was different.

To begin with, her hair was very curly. But worse still, it was bright *green*.

The King and Queen had tried everything — hair dyes, vitamins, special diets — but nothing seemed to work. They called in the Royal Hairdresser, the Royal Acupuncturist, the Royal Chiropractor, even the Royal Librarian, but none of them were able to suggest a cure. Princess Euphorbia's hair seemed determined to stay green.

Every night, as they climbed the steps into the Royal Feather Bed, they shook their heads sadly.

"What *are* we going to do?" asked King Eglantine. "She simply *must* produce a Royal Heir."

Lowly Assistant

Keeper of the Royal Chamber

Lord Protector of the Royal Teeth

Keeper of the Crown Jewels

Royal Hairdres

And Queen Gazania replied, "And I'd like some Royal Grandchildren too, Dear. But who will marry a princess with green hair?"

Before they went to sleep, they crossed their fingers, hoping that the princess's hair might change overnight to yellow or brown or red. But every morning, when she ran in to greet her parents, Euphorbia's hair was still the same, bright green.

One night, when they'd been worrying about it even more than usual, the King said, "Well, we could put an advertisement in the *Royal Gazette*, I suppose. Some kind-hearted prince might just happen to read it."

Royal Crown on Royal Wig

Royal Teeth

"It's certainly worth a try," said the Queen, balancing her crown on top of her hair curlers.

So the next morning, over muffins and marmalade, they wrote this advertisement.

Royal Gazette

Wanted — Prince,
Must have own Palace,
Coach and Horses, oh,
and Money.
Need Not be Handsome

After that, the Royal Telephone never stopped ringing and the Royal Doorbell never stopped clanging. But none of the princes were prepared to marry Euphorbia once they'd seen her.

Tea at the Palace

This went on for weeks until, one day, three princes arrived on the Royal Doorstep all at once.

The King and Queen were delighted and asked them in for tea in the Royal Parlor.

"Another cup?"

"No, thank you, Ma'am," said the first, Prince Pelargonium. "Pray, where is the enchanted wood I must chop down before I can marry your daughter, Sire?"

The second, Prince Laburnum, said, "King Eglantine, where is the fearsome dragon I must slay before I win your daughter's hand in marriage?"

And the third, Prince Nasturtium, said, "Where is the evil sorcerer I must outwit before you give me the Princess as my wife?"

But King Eglantine just laughed and said, "That's ridiculous!"

Queen Gazania said, "It's nonsense! We don't want a prince who'll go out killing dragons, chopping down forests, or outwitting sorcerers."

"No, we just want a prince with his own palace, coach, horses, and money, who's willing to marry Euphorbia," added King Eglantine.

So they rang for the Princess and she came skipping into the Royal Parlor, wearing a green dress, *and* green shoes, *and* green emeralds around her neck, *and* a green emerald tiara on her bright green hair.

The princes jumped to their feet in astonishment.

"Yuk!" said Prince Pelargonium. "Sorry, Your Majesties, must go. I promised Father I'd go dragon hunting with him this afternoon. Thanks for the muffins."

And Prince Laburnum said, "Blah! Sorry, Sire, but I've just remembered! My horse has a dental appointment. Must run. Thanks so much for the chocolate cake."

But Prince Nasturtium just stood transfixed, gazing at the Princess.

The King and Queen held their breath. No one had ever looked at Euphorbia like that before.

"He actually seems interested," whispered the King.

"I know, dear. Do you suppose it's love at first sight?"

"Maybe. But there's something odd about him," said the King. "He's a bit, well, greenish."

"Hush, dear, he's just a little pale. These lightbulbs need to be changed," said the Queen. "In any case, what do looks matter so long as he marries her?"

"Hark!" said Prince Nasturtium, falling to his knees at the Princess's feet. "Princess Euphorbia, wilt thou be mine?"

The Princess had never had a marriage proposal before. She was so surprised she didn't know what to say.

The King and Queen were stunned, of course, and asked gently, "Have you noticed the, er, color of her hair?"

"Oh, yes," said Prince Nasturtium. "It's my favorite. I'm an absolute greenie!"

So the King and Queen took Euphorbia aside and whispered that she'd better say yes quickly, before he had time to change his mind.

"Oh, very well," said Euphorbia. "He's quite cute, really."

She took a step toward Prince Nasturtium and was about to kiss him when he pulled away.

"Not now. Not before we're even engaged."

The Royal Wedding

The Palace announced the Royal Engagement. And what rejoicing there was! What preparation! What pictures! But not one picture of the new couple kissing. Prince Nasturtium had felt too embarrassed to kiss in public.

Roast
suckling
pig

Jellied
frogs' legs

Caviar

What a wedding! The bride wore green. The groom wore green. Even the King and Queen wore green.

And the wedding cake was covered in green icing.

Larks' tongues   Roast peacock

Royal Wedding Souvenirs

Royal We[dding] Remembra[nce]

Then Princess Euphorbia and Prince Nasturtium climbed into a green coach and drove off into the sunset.

All this time, the Princess had wanted to kiss her Prince, but he kept saying, "Please Euphorbia, not now. I've got a headache from all those Royal Trumpets."

But when they got to the Royal Honeymoon Hotel, she couldn't wait any longer and threw her arms around his neck and kissed him on the cheek.

Suddenly, there was a loud BANG! A flash of lightning! And lots and lots of green smoke. When it had all cleared away, there was no sign of Prince Nasturtium. He had vanished.

"Oh, rats!" said Euphorbia. "I knew it was too good to last. That Prince Nasturtium was just like the others. Mommy and Daddy are going to be awfully upset."

"Ribbit!" The noise came from down near her feet.

The Princess looked down and there, sitting on the floor, was a bright green frog.

Healthy
Royal
Snack

"What are you doing here?" asked the Princess. "Go away. Can't you see I'm sulking?"

But the frog croaked, "Beloved, it is I, Nasturtium. Don't you know me? You see, I used to be a frog, but a wicked witch turned me into a prince. Now, my darling, you have broken the spell and turned me back into a frog!"

Frog Flashback

Princess Euphorbia looked at him curiously. "You know, as a prince, you were only cute. As a frog, you're really special!"

And she picked him up and cuddled him.
"And what's even better is now you match
my hair."

"Ribbit."

So from then on, Princess Euphorbia and Nasturtium, her Royal Frog, lived more or less happily ever after.

And the King and Queen? Well, they had to be content with Royal Tadpoles for grandchildren.

the end

About the Author

Vashti Farrer

Vashti Farrer writes for adults and children in magazines and anthologies. She's had a picture book, novels, and plays published.

Her favorite hobby is reading, favorite color is purple, and favorite animal, cats. She's lived with birds, dogs, a tortoise, a rabbit, salamanders, a rat named Sigmund, and a possum named Milly. She now has a dog, two cats, and several possums as neighbors. She sometimes works as a movie extra.

About the Illustrator

Nan Bodsworth

Nan Bodsworth has written and illustrated four children's picture books. She has three grown-up children and two grand-daughters and lives at the beach near Geelong, Victoria, in Australia. She loves reading, daydreaming, making puppets, and snorkeling in the sea. Most of all, she likes looking at the world, which is full of interesting things.

Nan has always liked people better than animals. In fact, the only furry animals in her house are puppets, unless you count the occasional visiting mouse.